Collection of story

Children stories

Yuvrajsinh Jadav

ISBN 978-93-5458-691-0
© Yuvrajsinh Jadav 2021
Published in India 2021 by Pencil

Contributors:
Translator: Nishaba and nikulsinh

A brand of
One Point Six Technologies Pvt. Ltd.
123, Building J2, Shram Seva Premises,
Wadala Truck Terminal, Wadala (E)
Mumbai 400037, Maharashtra, INDIA
E connect@thepencilapp.com
W www.thepencilapp.com

DISCLAIMER: *This is a work of fiction. Names, characters,*

Author biography

Hello friends, Yuvraj Singh Jadav. I have brought a book for you today. This is my first book in Hindi. I have tried my best to like you. I have thought of helping you to tell your children stories to sleep at night. But, children do not like to hear the same story, so I have brought together seven new stories for you and your children. In which the battle of crows and caterpillars (Kamala) is my first story. Which I also like very much. So after reading this, you must reply to me. Friends, I am going to have my first novel later. So if you like these stories, then definitely read it.

CONTENTS

Preface

Golden spring....

A gigantic mountain called 'Jannat Pahad' and a beautiful stream flowing from it, but the stream had been flowing for many years and the surrounding area had become a dense forest of shrubs. The spring was flowing near a 'Sankat' village.

The people of Sankat village had never seen those springs. In order to escape the scorching heat of the summer season, all the people of that village came together and built a beautiful lake near the seam of Sankat village. Once there was a drought for three years in a row and the fourth year seemed to be coming. People were terrified because if it doesn't rain now, the villagers will starve to death.

At the same time a young man named 'Jay' who is loved by the people of the village. He told the villagers that a stream was flowing near our village. The spring water is very clean and drinkable. The villagers were happy and started walking with him. They all reached to the springs and drank its pure water. They drank the cool water of the spring and began to feel blessed.

At the same time, a sage named 'Krishnanath' with a big white beard like a big mountain in the Himalayas and the holy light of Lord Shankar's Kailash mountain came there and stopped him from drinking water, "Stop ... stop ...No one drink the water of this spring" . But the people of the village did not consider the sage a madman.

They took Jay and started dancing. Jai, you are our hero and you are the Messiha... all started chanting slogans happily. Now the people of the village began to live in peace. But it may not be pleasing by God, perhaps because of his happiness.

They started killing each other. Seeing people killing each other, Jai went to shock. He saw a beating between brother, he saw a beating between son & father. and he saw beating between husband and wife dying. He felt as if he had slipped into the abyss. He could not understand anything.

At the same time sage Krishnanath came to him and said "I tried to stop him but he did not believe me. This is a cursed spring. Its name is 'Golden Spring'. This spring flows from Jannat mountain. Blood is seen flowing in the water of these springs every :Poonam night'. Then the springs contain the 'Bhrata poison'. "

Jay asked, "Then it should be called a 'poisonous spring' or 'stream of blood'. So why is it called the 'Golden Spring'?

Then Krishnanath says, "You are right but the stone inside these springs is of gold. Hence it is called the 'Golden Spring'.

Jay was shocked! He asked the sage, "this spring is golden

then who cursed it? Why?

Then sage Krishnanath reveals his secret to answer his question: -

Long ago it was a beautiful town on a 'Jannat Pahad'. The name of the city was 'Golden', and the city was full of gold. It was as beautiful as heaven and cool as Mountain Kailash. The king of 'Surabhadravanshi' ruled for a long time in that golden city. Longevity was a great and learned king. He saw God in the guest and considered the younger people of his kingdom as his son, respected the older one and was a charismatic king. His army was the strongest, the people in his kingdom were happy and healthy. He established monastery there to acquaint the people with knowledge. In which a person is motivated to work hard and eat.

People were recognizable from their work. The one who blends in protection is called 'Kshatriya', the one who performs Yagna is called 'Brahman', the one who trades in commerce is called 'Vaishya' and the one who performs less and less than them is called 'Shudra'. Those people were happy in their deeds. Brotherhood in the whole town, no one was aware of brother-brother or any other kind of quarrel. Everyone was ready to help each other.

He considered the people of the town to be gods. He was considered a virtuous person. Where no one knows happiness or sorrow. He was absorbed only in work, brotherhood, and pleading with God. So that they would not have time for anything other than that.

The main reason for the beauty of the golden city was the spring of that city. Whose name was the 'Golden Spring'. That canal was founded by a king named Surabhadra. He came to live with his family on King Jannat mountain. He and his family dug a river called 'Lavanya' and rescued canal. That canal was confined to that town only. So that the water in the town was gone forever.

There was also a kingdom against the Golden city kingdom and its king was Yamanraj. He was very greedy and cruel. He was the most cruel and diplomatic king of the Krunal dynasty. As soon as he became king, he first met his father Majmuddar in jail. So that it does not interfere with his work. The whole town was horrified. People were introduced to the word 'slave'.

Then he had a strong desire to acquire the vast state golden city in front of him to develop the state. Because it was a very golden and happy state with a golden stream flowing in it. However, the state had a large army. So he took the help of a mahant sage Atri. He lied to the sage, "I want to move my state forward, to develop. If you help me, he won't starve. " The sage, seeing his feelings for the people and public welfare, went to talk to him.

He set out on a journey to the Golden City. The king of the city of gold was a Dirghayu king. He was the son of Surabhadra. He was a heroic and valiant king. The kings who came against him were always defeated. He fought many battles and was victorious. Even the gods were afraid of his might. He respected the sages. The people in his kingdom were happy. The king bowed to Atri. Atri was happy and Yamanraj came as Atri's disciple. He was watching the state. He saw the army of Dirghayu and got his general with him. His name was Parasitic. The general said that Dirghayu goes to Mahadev temple on Poonam for Shivayacha the next day and he will return on the third day. Yamanraj started a war on Poonam and betrayed and killed the Dirghayu's family.

When the Dirghayu was informed, he left the newborn son he had brought with him in the Mahadev temple at the foot of Jannat Pahad and the king made a mark on his body to identify him. Sage Atri was also with the Dirghayu and he warned Yamanraj, as well as asked him to return the kingdom. Yamanraj was proud to see the prowess of his family and sons. It soon invaded on Dirghayu. Dirghayu fought very valiantly. He fought alone and frightened Yamanraj, but the son of Paravalambi struck later and Dirghayu fell in love by death.

Seeing this, sage Atri became angry and took the water of the "golden" spring flowing there and cursed it. He has done injustice because of these springs and because of his own greed. By lying to me, a war broke out behind Dirghayu and unknowingly made me a partner in this sin. So I curse you that whoever drinks the water of this spring will fight with each other and die like an animal. "

The next day, the fighting started in the town. Brother-brother, father-son, husband-wife and thus the whole town came to an end. The survivors came down to the Mahadev temple here. He never drank the water of that spring again.

Hearing this, Jay asked the sage Krishnanath: "So the curse of these springs can never be erased and even an innocent man who takes its water will fall victim to it? Won't the people of my village be free from the curse? "Krishnanath replies: "When many years have passed. Then many sages and new comers to the town approached sage Atri and started begging for some remedy to take back the curse of this spring or destroy it. Now, those people have died and the city of Golden city has become a ruin. The trees in that place have also dried up.

Then the sage remembered the son of Dirghayu and his descendants. He said, "Only when the Dirghayu's son becomes the king of this city and he could the 'Bhrata canal', the 'bharta poison' will be destroyed from the water of this spring."

Hearing this, Jay leaves for Jannat Pahad. He leaves with the blessings of Krishnanath and the people of his village in different cages. The sage hired his disciples to take care of him and he too goes out to jannat mountain with Jay. He says that when the curse of these springs is destroyed, those people will regain their lost votes.

Now, as he headed towards Jannat Pahad, Jay first remembered that Mahadev temple. Jay said to Krishnanath, "You said that there is a mark on his son's body. Do you know. Krishnanath was also happy to hear that & told him that he don't know but the priest of the temple must know. He then reached the temple and worshiped the Shivling. Responding to sage Krishnanath and Jay, the priest say that he drew 'Trishul' on the body of the child. While Jay also had 'Trishul' on his body.

So, he was made the king of the golden city and then 'Bhrata canal' was performed. In which he found peace in the souls of the fathers and the golden spring became golden again. The people of his village were also freed from the curse and came to live in the golden city.

Thus, in the end, the truth prevailed.

Author: Yuvraj Singh Jadav

Battle of crows and caterpillars..

The story began in the jungle. In which there was a big mango tree on the bank of Shravan river. Its name was Amrapallava. It was a beautiful caterpillar palace on a tree. His king's name was Satyapallava. He was truthful and intelligent, he had many valiant soldiers and even an old man who used Chanakyaniti. Those old caterpillars were teaching all caterpillars discipline and weaponry. The caterpillars lived on that tree and around it. Every caterpillar worked hard. He was eating his own right. Everyone, including the king, was busy with different things. Whenever there was a problem, they would all come together and face the problem together.

The summer season had begun. At that time the same forest was ruled by crows. After all, they were birds and they flew everywhere to find water. He was also a king of crows, he was very lazy and arrogant. For them the summer season was an opportunity to rule the whole forest. Although the summer season always came but at that time the forest was ruled by vultures but now they are extinct.

So that the crows were getting taller. His cruel king was called Kagsinh in the forest, accompanied by three other crows as strong and intelligent as him, including Kagsinh's confidant 1. Kagabhadra, then 2. more intelligent ones, Kagkendra and 3. more powerful ones, Kagabalendra. The four of them ruled over the other crows together. However, Kagsingh had all these qualities, so he was a king.

Several days later a crow saw the Shravan river and also saw the trees on its banks where even in the scorching heat there was a feeling of winter chill. Seeing this, the crow went to the cruel king Kagsingh and talked to him about the river Shravan. Hearing this, the hot crows reached the bank of Shravan river with him. There he began to drink water. After drinking the water, all the crows started flying around. When he reached the tree, he saw a palace of caterpillars. So that they stopped flying there.

Kagasinh sent a message through his soldiers. The crow's messenger reached the caterpillar's palace and began to read the message sent by the crow. In which it was written, "King Kagsingh of the whole forest has come before you today. He wants to exercise his power over your kingdom and you cater to all the caterpillars. We will not attack you but will protect you. If you want war we will give you two days then we will attack you."

Hearing this message, an atmosphere of grief prevailed entire in the Amrapallavanagar. The towns people began to prepare for battle. But at that time his king Satyapallava and the wise elders there convened a meeting. Began to take their votes, including an old man named Kirtikant who removed a lot of trouble from his intellect. "As long as there is unity among the crows, we will not be able to win. That is why they have to fight each other first." He said.

Then the next day was night time. The meeting was over. There was silence in the whole state. Fear gripped the town. At that time King Satyapallav asked Kirtikant,"why this cruel king who came in front of us was called 'Kag Singh', 'Singh'?

Then Kirtikant says, "A long time ago, the crow was born in a cruel prison. In which his mother educated him and after he became a little young, he and his mother cleverly came out without being seen by the vulture and this crow and his mother were called great. ”

But the crow was never persuaded by his mother to work and eat. So his mother always had to arrange the meal. Once time his mother's health deteriorated. So the crow has to go out for a meal. He wanders in the forest all day but no finds food anywhere, he returns home disappointed. There he sees the battle of the great lion and there are two lions fighting face to face for the kingdom and one of the lions is very wounded and he is defeated. At that moment, the crow had an idea that after the death of this lion, I would make it a meal.

After a while the crow chases after him and waits for his death, after a while the crow starts biting at the lion's bite. The lion gets angry but can't catch the crow. Taking advantage of this, the crow beats the lion to death. Eventually the crow goes to his mother with the flesh of his dying flesh. His mother was shocked to see him. The

crow's body was covered in blood. His mother started asking him, "What happened son ..."
Before he could speak further, the haughty crow said, "Today I hunted a lion so that my whole day was spent in killing it."

Hearing this, his sick mother sat up in amazement. His mother told this to the crows around him, but they laughed and asked him for proof. Then the crow blew them all away. They were also surprised to see a dead lion as only a crow's beak was visible on the body of that lion. He had his beak killed every time he touched the body of that lion. So all the crows gave him the title of killing a lion and gave him the name "Lion" behind the crow as a gift.

Kirtikant says that: - This is how the crow got the title of lion.

Satyapallava then walked into his room. Now, Satyapallava's sleep was also blown away. When Kirtikant goes to his house and uses his Chanakya intellect. He was first of all his heroic grand son whose name was Shorya. Whose merits sang the whole kingdom. His grandfather Kirtikant tells him "You are not going to war." On hearing this, Shorya became angry and told his grandfather, "This is not our heritage. Many years ago my parents also laid down their lives for freedom and now when it is our turn, you not allowed me to fight. The king and all the people have undoubted faith in you and me. If we die in the war, then horrified will be scared in the state." Then his grandfather told him to calm down; Not going to be a war before. Shorya was stunned to hear this. Hearing that,

Shorya asked, "What's going to happen first?"

Then Kirtikante says: - You will know tomorrow what we will do tomorrow, but today and now at night you should go to the poisonous forest far away from here, arrive as soon as possible. Go there and pick up a snake-shaped herb leaf and bring it. Bring it and mix it in our huge bathroom. " Shorya was asked by her grandfather to ask a single question. Now, he takes a few soldiers and leaves to fill the containers.

The next day the sun came out like a black light. The citizens of the town also came to the battlefield with weapons for their freedom. Everyone was there at that time but King Satyapallava and Kirtikant were neither of them. After a while king and Kirtikant came there and he said to Kagsinh "We accept your offer of slavery. But in your kingdom you are four heroes, means four kings. But we will enslave any one of you. Kagsingh was happy to hear that and said to him "Yes! I also want you all to be my slaves. " Hearing this, his other three friends got angry and opposed Kagsingh. Angered by this, Kagsingh sentenced all three of them and their accomplices to death so that a distance war broke out between the crows.

In which three heroic crows and their accomplices were killed. So the crow and the caterpillar did not fight that day. But there was a war between crows and crows, which made the caterpillars happy.

In the evening, Shorya with his army reached Amrapallava with a serpent. When he found out about this, there was an atmosphere of happiness in the town. At that time Kirtikant came and mixed the poison in the bath there. At the behest of Kirtikant, each caterpillar bathed in it. Gathering all the caterpillars, he showed the greatness of unity for the last time and said, "We have broken the unity of those crows today. So that victory will be ours."

The next day all the caterpillars were ready to fight against Kagsingh. Angered by this betrayal, the crows descended on the battlefield. Those crows ate all the caterpillars. So eager to eat happily. When the caterpillars came all bathing. The battle began and each crow picked up the caterpillars and began to eat them. In a few moments the crows began to die. Seeing this, Kagsingh got scared and fled from there. The caterpillar was victorious and happily came to Amrapallav.

If Kagsingh had these three intelligent and strong crows he could have won this battle.

Therefore, Kirtikant broke their unity and won.

Thus, even the impossible can be done with intelligence.

Gigo..

One day I was quietly going out for my work. At that time one thief came to me and showed me a knife and said, "Bring what you have."

I was surprised to see the knife. I gave him everything and then asked "Who are you brother?"

So he laughed and said "I" laughed again and said "I am a robber and I have come to rob your thing." It was then that I remembered my grand mother saying. "In the Bhagavad Gita, Lord Krishna says (there is nothing wrong with eating it now) that mean 'live with as they are.' So I rob his thing too.
All the friends sitting next to Giga, started laughing and said just such a big punishment for that.

Gigo, a friend sitting next to him, said: 'Brother, what are you talking about?'

Now Gigo spoke: "Brother, then brought me to the police station and took me to court on the third day."

Jigo spoke again: "What are doing in between one day."Gigo looked at and said, "Don't talk about it. The mosquitoes died in this prison at midnight all day. The mosquitoes died in this prison and the rest went to someone else's room with their belongings." Everyone laughed.

Jigo said, "But why did the judge punish you so severely?"

Gigo 'Yes! Let's go in flash back.'

When I was taken to court, I was there, there was a judge and there was a policeman, but there was a robber?

Everyone was shocked!

Gigo said "Yes! I was shocked too."

Then the lawyer came. He kept asking me questions. Lawyer's first question: "Where did you meet that thief?"

Gigo's answer: "No, I didn't go to see him."

Lawyer's second question: "So why did you give him money?"

Giga's answer: "That is what he asked from me."

Lawyer's third Question: "Didn't you know he was a thief or a robber?"

Giga's answer: "No."

Lawyer's fourth question: "When did you find out?"

Giga's answer: "When I asked his name, he told me that, he was a thief. At first I also laughed and said talk to you aunty, no give such a foolish this name. So, he got angry and told me, "I told my job, I was a thief." So I told him, " Did you know that, i asked your name. So you give me the answer". You have not been given a sacrament. So he got angry.

Lawyer's fifth question: "What did you do then?"

Giga's answer: "First I thought, then I got the idea that my mother used to say, in Srimad Bhagavad Gita, Sri Krishna has said 'live with them as they are' so I also stole his thing."

Lawyer's sixth question: "What was it?"

Giga's answer: "His knife!"

Lawyer's seventh question: "What did you do with it after then?"

Giga's answer: "After the knife was cut, there was nothing worth doing."

Lawyer's last question: "So you mean he got scared or ran away?"

Giga's answer: "No, I just hit him so hard that he lost consciousness."

"My lord, hit him so hard that he died."

The lawyer spoke in his argument.

There was silence throughout the court. As it is in you right now. Gigo fell silent as Giga's mouth closed.
So, Jiga asked one more question: "So the judge sentenced you immediately.
On hearing this"

Gigo said, "No, he is called a judge, a judge who weighs injustice and justice, so he also asked questions."

Judge's first question: "Isn't stealing the life of that thief a crime?"

Giga's answer: "Yes."

Judge's second question: "should you be punished?"

Giga's answer: "No."

Judge's third question: "Why?"

Upon hearing this, Giga asked the judge permission to ask questions.

Giga's first question: "He tried to rob me. Isn't that a crime?"

Judge's Answer: "Yes."

Gigo's second question: "So, why punish me with one?"

Judge's answer: "Because, the thief was given the same punishment by you."

Gigo's third question: "So, you punish him?"

Judge's answer: "Yes, give it!"

Gigo's fourth question: "You didn't like it because, I punishment to him ....?"

On hearing this, the whole court started laughing as well as the lawyer of Giga's counterpart started laughing. So, the judge took the hammer lying next to him and reprimanded him.

Judge Punch repeatedly asked, "No, not like this, but you gave him a big punishment to him?"

Gigo spoke: "He was also robbed of my money. Is it anything less?"

The judge said: "Rupees will be found again, but life is found only once."

Gigo spoke: "No, my grand mother refused and said 'no'. If you lose this money, you will never find once again."

Now everyone laughing in the court and here Jigo grabbed his stomach and started laughing.

Gigo (came out of the conversation) said: "The judge not asked a question and allowed me to go by crazy, but I don't think it's acceptable because he called crazy & send to me in a bunch of crazy people who don't even know how to wash."

Jigo spoke: "What did you say?"

Gigo spoke: "I made the same request with both hands. 'Hey! Judge, send me in to a bunch the madman who know to wash the same."

Hearing this, the jail soilders laughed also who standing near the gate.

Unity there domination..

In one village lived six blind men. One long, one short, one has a big nose, one thick, one thin and one has a long toothed. They was heard name of the elephants but, being blind, they could not see them (the elephants) and every day they would discuss the same elephant and finally they would have to drop the discussion.

One day they went out to satisfied their curiosity. They went to the elephant herd in the village. That armed brother had gone to the village for some reason.

So, without waiting for the man they went to the elephant, & they started touching it. The Long man began to move his hand on the elephant's tail, the thin man began to touch ears, the long-toothed man began to touch it on the back, the short man began to touch its trunk and the big man began to touch its legs. They began to describe shape of the elephant.

Long man said: "This elephant is like a rope."

Thin said: "No. This elephant is like a huge space. "

The toothman said: "This elephant is like a wall."

Short man said: "No. This elephant is like a dragon. "

The thick-nosed said: "This elephant is like the trunk of a tree."

Eventually their opinions differed, and they began to quarrel with each other. Their quarrel intensified. The stone turned on all fours. So the armed came their. He was furious to see all this.

The owner of the elephant said (loudly), "Stop."

Hearing his voice, Long man said, "Brother! This elephant is like a rope!"

Thin man said: "This elephant is like a rope!"

Once again, they began to disagree. So the brother said, "You are all wrong. You are all blind. None of one had seen the elephant. So how do you know what it looks like or what its shape is?"

"If you really want to see the shape of that elephant, you have to get each other's opinions together."
Thus, we are just as blind to religion. If we are to see that (God-like) elephant, we must all agree on each other's opinions. Then we can go and see that (God-like) elephant. (Can be experienced).
That is why its said: - Unity is domination there.

Death or cat..

There was a one grocery store in the town. A lot of rats living in that grocery store. The food in that shop was plentiful for them. They ate everything and spoiled all the bags of food growing. Also spoiled the shop's bread, biscuits and fruit.

The grocer got really worried. So, he thought, "I should buy a cat and let it stay in the grocery store. Only then can I save my things."

He bought a nice, fat cat and kept it in the store. The cat had a great time hunting and killing rats. She daily killed and ate one or two rats. Mice can no longer roam freely in that shop. They were afraid that the cat would kill them at any moment.

One mouse wanted to do something. They held a meeting and all said the same thing, "We must get rid of the cat." So an old rat said, "Can anyone give a suggestion?"

All the mice sat up and nodded. One smart looking rat stood up and said, "The cat moves slowly. This is the problem. If we can tie a bell around its neck, things will be fine. We will be able to know the cat's movements."

"Yeah, we have the same answer," all the mice seem to say. An old rat slowly stood up and asked, "Who will ring the bell?" After a few moments there was no one to answer the question.

·

·

·

Whatever we are, we have to accept it because when God takes the form of a dead cat, who will ring the bell?

The anguish of Parrot-Mena's love

In a beautiful forest, the two lovers- petals Parrot and Mena lived their. They was very happy. They were living a life of wandering and playing together. One day, Mena asked to the parrot, "You not leave me and fly away? Right..."

Parrot : "If I fly, you will catch me."

Mena : "I can catch you, but I can't get you."

Tears welled up in the parrot's eyes, when he heard that.

Soon after, the parrot cut off theirs wings and said to Mena, "Now we will always be together."

One day, there was a storm in the forest. Large mountain-like shrubs began to collapse. Seeing that, Parrot and Mena started flying.

The parrot said to Mena : "I can't fly. You go.."

Hearing that, Mena flew away immediately.
When the storm subsided, Mena saw that parrot die on a tree and he wrote on a branch."

It simply came to our notice then
I can't leave you,
So maybe the storm came
I am not dead before.

"Author: Yuvraj Singh Jadav

Precious gifts..

One day a small child named Chiranjeev was living in a beautiful house. His mom and dad teased him. Not even letting him for play. But every day he would hear a fairy's story near from his grand mother. One day, Chiranjeev's one teeth fell out and he remembered the fairy tale he had left. He fell a sleep with his teeth under his pillow. Early the next morning, a fairy came to Chiranjeev and asked him, "What do you want, Chiranjeev?"

Chiranjeev says; "Fun and fun."

The fairy says, "I will give you not one but four precious gifts. I will take your parents in return."
Chiranjeev was happy. He had more fun and now he will be able to live life without any disturbing and will also get four precious gifts from above.

When the fairy thought and say to him for the first precious gift. Then he was a small child, so he began to say to the fairy, "I must have fun, what are the thinking about it." Then the fairy gave him laughter and merriment and the fairy disappeared. Then he came back and had a lot of fun. After a few years, he got tired by running around and now he started doing aphasos.
Then Chiranjeev sits alone and sad and thinks that it

would have been better if I said for the love. In a few moments the fairy came again with a chhab in front of her and her chhab now had four gifts and he demanded love from her. Give him a beautiful woman for love and the fairy disappears again.

Chiranjeev was very happy and love came into his life. He got a beautiful girlfriend and they got married. After a while they started arguing and he got frustrated again.

Now, Chiranjeev regrets that he was disappointed by his wife's harassment. He began to think, I already had to seek fame. In a few days the fairy came again and asked Chiranjeev for her gift. Chiranjeev spoke immediately I need fame. The fairy laughed again and gave him the gift of glory.

Chiranjeev now became a man of fame. Everyone started respecting him. He was happy but one day a one king kicked him and moved away. He sent soilders behind him saying that just being famous will not forgive your tax.

Chiranjeevi again remembered one last gift to the fairy. As soon as the fairy came to him, he demanded wealth from her. The fairy told him to think again. But Chiranjeev did not believe and finally demanded wealth fom him. He is now a wealthy man. People began to respect him again.

Now Chiranjeev had everything. But still he was not happy. Who knows who noticed his happiness. Once time he finds a happy and prosperous man like him. He is amazed to see her. Then he asks, "Did the fairy gave you a precious gift?"

The man replied with a laugh," Yes!"

Chiranjeevi asked the man again, "Are you really happy as you look?"

The man said with laugh, "why did you asked me this question?"

Then Chiranjeev asked, "Really, I have every thing, yet..." He got stuck and see two old couples in front of him. They was Chiranjeev's parents.

Seeing them, Chiranjeev asked the man a question, "What gift did you took from the fairy?"

Then the man says, "look in front ... that old couple appears. I asked the fairy mommy-daddy who gave it to me."

Curry mash and sweet neem

While inside the prison Mistan made curry and mash(khichdi). At that time only neem leaves were visible in the curry. What a wonderful way to screw people over. Gigo even bit the leaf like a buffalo. But soft Jigo did not consider it edible. When he came back to his room on the ground, Jigo looked at Giga and asked a question.

"Why do you mix sweet neem in this curry?"
Gigo laughed and said, "Why should a goat wants pudding in its mouth?"

Jigo swelled his nose and spoke. "You are like a buffalo ... so everything goes awry. I don't feel like squeezing this curry every Wednesday and even in this, this neem is as big as a mound.""Who made this food? "
Gigo responds. "I am more intelligent than you. I asked this question to my mother when I was only seven years old."

"What did your mother say?"

"He told me the whole story."

"I must also hear the story, who made this curry paste and the practice of sweet neem?"

Gigo, like a yogi sitting in meditation, lifts both legs over each other and takes a few long breaths and said "then listen"

In the deep forest a king named Surajmal was ruling in a town. On the night of Ashadhi, the queen of Surajmal gave birth to two twin daughters. At that time the rains came for fifteen consecutive days and the lives of the people were in danger in the flood situation. So King Surajmal and all the others fell in charge of the kingdom. No one acknowledge the king's two daughters. When the flood of continuous rain is over, the king goes to the queen. Surajmal asks the maids to bring their daughters to see. At that time a one maid goes to the queen to take her princesses. Then the second maid standing next to the queen says like joking.

"Which princess does the king want to see first? Just ask."

The maid who came to take the princesses went to the king and told him this. Now, the issue was whether the children were younger or older. The princesses were not named. By the time of their sixth(naming day), the whole state was in an uproar. Due to which he could not pay attention on his princesses. So the king could not say anything and got angry with the joke made by the queen and forbade the naming of both the princess.
The maid went and told the queen. The queen was saddened and punished the teasing maid. The queen apologizes to the maharaja(king) and speaks of naming her princesses. Then Surajmal says.

"Now I will name my princesses by their own skill."

The king's decision was final. At the age of eighteen, both princesses completed their studies. Both the princesses were very fond of cooking. One day the two princesses invented a new dish with the idea of cooking something new. One princess made a new dish by mixing mugi dal and rice, adding salt and turmeric and boiling it. The princess named it "Khichdi" and with it the princess got the title of Khichdi as the researcher of Khichdi. But one day his other twin sister told the princess to kill the wax.

"This is for the old man and the young man for the sake of this mess of yours."

So the princess mixed turi dal and rice to make a new kheechadi called "Vaghareli kheechadi".

Khichdi's other sister was also researching a new dish. So one day he took chana flour

Gigo says stepping out of the story.

"This is how curry and kheechadi were born to two beautiful princesses."

Jigo takes Giga back to the story (showing Giga with the salty lemon-covered twig in his mouth.)"

How did Giga mix this sweet lemon in this?"

"It simply came to our notice then. Let's get back to that

story. ” Gigo seemed to shine.

At the time of the princess's birth, two children were born to a doctor in the same state on the same day in the middle of the night. They both named it Neem. The doctor sends his children to learn medicine when they grow up. From there the two returned to learn medicine and at the same time brought together the research of the plant they had done.

People look at their plants and say.

"Both of these neems have brought a new tree and they have named their plant after their own name."Both neems were happy, so a crooked old man from the crowd spoke.

"Which of the two is better?"

That old man's question is also appropriate. With that in mind, the two brothers left the decision of their neem superiority to others. People tried to learn to use their neem. One of them had neem leaves (salt). Which was of no use. But because its neem is sweet, it is also known as "salt neem".

While the other brother's neem leaves were bitter. But his place in medicine became inferior. As the mosquitoes got away from the smoke of its leaves, people found it very useful. Therefore, it was recognized as a bitter neem as well as an honor of excellence.

In time, bitter neem became arrogant. Her marriage also

ended soon. People started wow ... wow.

He was proud of his neem and his work. The respect of the sweet neem was diminished. No one even believed in his medical knowledge and began to insult him.

One day King Surajmal formed a swayamvar to find a suitable groom for his daughters. In which young cooks or any educated people who are immersed in this innovative dish cooked by their princess are invited to participate. It also had many outside princes, scholars also took part in it and two of the nine young men in their kingdom were medical experts. Sweet neem and bitter neem began to be praised as soon as they entered.

People thought of the bitter neem, 'Today he might marry the same princess.'

The contest was started. Each contestant tried to blend into their dish using their own special item. If someone tried to get it out, someone got mixed up. Due to which Raja Surajmal also had a fear of declaring the husband of the two sisters as the successor of this kingdom.

At the same time, the first bitter neem came with its own dish. He had dipped his own neem leaves in the curry. People were doing 'Jai Jai Kar' of bitter neem. Hearing his Jai Jai Kar, the king felt it was right to be the same king. In a few minutes, his dish was given to the Kadhi Princess "Kadhi" mixed with bitter neem leaves. The princess put a spoon in the mouth of the curry and immediately removed it by saying "thu ... thu ... thu ..."

However, there was no confusion inside the mash. The bitter neem was disappointed and went back. King Surajmal was also concerned. Now the king and the people thought that the swayamvar of the princesses would fail. So Swayamvara was just about to complete it when a sweet neem came there by mixing its neem leaves in a curry. Her curry was taken to Princess 'Kadhi'. The princess tasted the curry as before and drank all the curry she had brought to her.

Princess 'Khichdi' also tasted her curry which she also found very tasty and mixed it with curry mixed with sweet neem.

The king and the people understood. Only sweet neem is now fit to be the successor of this state.

Thus, sweet neem mixed with curry and mash. The practice has been around ever since.

Hearing Giga's story, Jiga's mouth watered and he got up from there and started eating curry paste and sweet neem again in the kitchen.